This book belongs to...

Bertie's challenge... Can you find the chicks on every page?

For Mum & Dad - My Heroes - K.R.
For My Parents- My Mentors - A.N.

Bertie The Balloon at the Farm first published by Kim Robinson and Aneta Neuman
This edition published 2016
Text copyright © Kim Robinson 2009
Illustrations © Aneta Neuman 2016

Printed in Poland
www.djaf.pl
ISBN 978-0-9934627-2-6

www.bertietheballoon.com
Bertietheballoon@hotmail.com

Written by
Kim Robinson

Illustrated by
Aneta Neuman

Bertie The Balloon at the Farm

Bertie is a **BIG**, red, shiny balloon.
He's round, squishy and shaped like the mooh.

Bertie can fly high up in the sky,
Higher than the trees - oh MY, oh MY!

How lucky that he is so light and FREE
As balloons are filled with air, you see.

But, be careful Bertie, don't get swept away.
The wind's a dangerous place for you to play.

Bertie has a secret he wants to share with you.
Not only does he fly, but he can talk, too!

For Bertie is a magical balloon
Who goes on adventures, as you'll see soon.

Bertie lives in the country with his new friend May
In a **big** farmhouse, where they laugh and play.

Today he is going to help on the farm.
May has promised him he'll come to no harm.

At 6am he hears a
cockle doodle doo

Followed shortly by a baa baa,
a cluck and a mOO.

It's first to the chickens
to collect the eggs.

Next to milk the cows, a bucket
under their legs.

Then to the horses to feed them fresh hay,
They gobble it up eagerly. "Yum yum, neigh neigh."

Off to the goats, with a handful of weed
Then finally to the pigs,
who look VERY
hungry indeed!

The animals were happy now they had been fed.
"What's next on the list?" Bertie cheerfully said.

"Rounding up the sheep," May replied with a smile.
So holding Bertie tight,
she SkIpPeD
to the fence stile.

But as she climbed over the break in the wall,
she slipped and towards the ground she did fall.

Standing up, she brushed the dirt from her hair.
"Oh NO. Where's Bertie?" she said,
but he wasn't there.

As Bertie sailed away over the lush green meadows
He saw a funny looking man who was covered in crows.

"HELP me," he shouted,
but poor Bertie he
did ignore
Because it was
only a scarecrow,
stuffed full of
straw!

Suddenly from below him Bertie heard a commotion.
The crows in the field swarmed up like a black ocean.

They covered the sky like **WAVES** in the sea
"Oh no," screamed Bertie. "They're heading towards me."

Before he could move, they were pecking his cheeks.
"Ouch," screamed Bertie. "You have very
sharp beaks."

They **CLAWED** at his string and sat on his head.
"Get off me," he shouted, his voice full of dread.

Worried he would burst, Bertie could take no more,
So mustering up all his strength, he let out
a huge "ROAR".

The birds looked scared and flew quickly away.
"That was close," he said. "What an awful display!"

Then out of the blue, the wind suddenly dropped.
Confused, Bertie shook his head, "Oh, I've stopped!"

Falling towards the ground, he landed with a thud.
"Ouch," exclaimed Bertie. "I'm all covered in **MUD**!"

"Oh no, not the pigpen," he said with a frown.
No longer red, he was now covered in **brown**.

The pigs looked at him and let out a "snort".
This was one adventure Bertie wanted to abort.

He **SQUELCHED** and **slipped**
his way to the gate.
He wished he was back in the arms of his mate.

"Pwoahh. What's that smell?" asked an
embarrassed Bertie.
'No way. It's me," he blushed. "I'm so very, very dirty!"

Looking around, he spied
a water tank.
So he bounced over,
JuMpEd in and sank.

He splashed and swirled
until the mud disappeared.
"I'm shiny once again,"
Bertie smiled and cheered.

Bertie felt happy now
he was scrubbed clean,
So he drifted in the wind to
a field of green.

Settling on the grass, he curled up in a heap
And by counting sheep, he drifted off to sleep. Z..z..Z..z..

But, Bertie didn't realise the field was occupied
By a BIG, brown bull who was very
tall and w i d e.

The bull puffed, panted and pawed at the ground.
How dare someone impose on his personal surround?

With a MASSIVE snort and a
hearty grunt
The bull raced forward towards his hunt.

With his razor sharp horns
pointed straight at Bertie
The bull was determined to play dirty.

Closing in, the balloon just metres away,
The bull laughed,
"This is going to make my day!"
But just as the bull was about to strike
A small boy rode past the meadow on his bike.

"Oh dear," shouted the little stranger.
"Get up, balloon," he screamed. "You're in real
danger."
Bertie opened his eyes and sat up in a fluster
And on spying the bull,
all his strength he did muster.

Bertie swayed sideways trying to catch the breeze
To be safe he needed to be as high as the trees.

Slowly, but surely he rose up into the sky
Just in time to see the angry bull race by.

Shaking like jelly,
Bertie drifted towards to road.

He was Jumping so much,
he looked like a toad!

"Thank you so very much,"
said Bertie to the lad.

"You're welcome", he replied.
"That bull looked so mad!"

"This farm has many dangers for a red balloon like me."
"The mud, the crows, the bull", sniffed Bertie, woefully.

"Then come home with me," replied Jack full of JOY.
"I need a new friend",
thought Bertie, looking at the boy.

"Wow," shouted Bertie. "What a brilliant idea."
"I'm Jack," he said. "I don't live far from here."
Now safe and secure with his brand new mate.
"It's time for a new ADVENTURE,"
Bertie cheered. "And I can't wait!"

THE END

Look out for Bertie's next adventure...

Bertie The Balloon at the Circus...
Coming soon!

Also available to buy NOW...
Bertie The Balloon at the Fairground
&
Bertie The Balloon at the Zoo

Rated 5 Stars on amazon.co.uk

"Delightfully engaging and colourful children's books."
"Bertie is fantastic."
"Great books of rhyming with wonderful illustrations."
"These books are amazing. Highly recommended."
"Children absolutely adore these books."
"Awesome read!"
"Beautiful pictures & lovely rhyming storylines."

Now it's your turn to colour Bertie!